Children's Books:
Who Needs Teeth?

Sally Huss

ISBN: 0692351191
ISBN 13: 9780692351192

Who needs teeth?

If a rabbit didn't have teeth with which to chew,

He wouldn't be able to eat carrots like you.

A dog without teeth couldn't chew on a bone.

And a cat without teeth would be so messy

that she'd have to eat alone.

A cow without teeth couldn't chew on her cud

That would leave her hungry, standing in the mud.

A horse loves to graze on grass,

But without teeth his grazing wouldn't last.

Who else needs teeth? What about you?

Are there some things you like to chew too?

If you didn't have teeth, you wouldn't have fun.

You couldn't eat an apple or a cinnamon bun.

You couldn't eat a sandwich made of cheddar cheese.

You couldn't eat your vegetables like green beans or peas.

You couldn't eat all the things that make you strong and bright.

You couldn't eat a snack in the middle of the night.

You couldn't celebrate Thanksgiving by eating turkey

and pumpkin pie.

You'd have to drink a smoothie and say, "That's fine."

But it would be a lie.

You couldn't eat a birthday cake on your special day.

You'd be left with only ice cream, as they'd take the cake away.

You couldn't eat bananas without choking on the lumps.

You couldn't eat cherries without seeming to have the mumps.

You couldn't eat a sandwich made of jelly and peanut butter.

You'd have to have it blended, but that wouldn't make it better.

You couldn't eat marshmallows from a stick.

Your mouth would fill, but the marshmallows would stick.

You couldn't eat a cookie, so you need not worry about the crumbs.

And you couldn't eat fruits with pits like peaches, apricots,

or plums.

You couldn't sink your teeth into a foamy lemon meringue pie.

You'd have to watch the others eat it, which might make you cry.

Then too, if you didn't have teeth you wouldn't want to smile.

That might not bother you for just a little while.

But if you're a happy kid who likes to smile, have friends,

and run and play,

You might just want to find a way to help your teeth to stay.

For teeth are like people, they like to be loved and cared for.

It is not a lot to ask for all the work they are there for.

They are there to chew your food,

Which keeps you healthy and in a good mood.

It takes a little time to care for them and keep them clean.

It is something you must learn to do, if you want them to be seen.

For a smile is like a postcard, a welcome sign to others,

To let them know you're friendly and would like them

as sisters and brothers.

So keep your toothbrush handy and your toothpaste close by too,

And brush your teeth each morning and night

and see what that will do.

A happy face starts with a very happy smile.

And a happy smile is filled with happy teeth to make

a happy, healthy child.

Who needs teeth?

You need teeth!

We all need teeth!

The end,
but not the end
of caring
for your teeth.

At the end of this book you will find a Certificate of Merit that may be issued to any child who honors the requirements stated in the Certificate. This fine Certificate will easily fit into a 5"x7" frame, and happily suit any child who receives it!

Here is another fun, rhyming book by Sally Huss.

Synopsis: A very stubborn, bored, and uninspired cow is steadfast in her determination not to try something new. She is amusingly invited to join one animal after the next in an adventure, but sticks to her old habits. It is not until a chicken encourages her to jump over the moon that she decides to change her ways and try something new.

All in rhyme, and all with a smile, this story is one to delight every child, and subtly spark the spirit of adventure within them. It emphasizes the importance of trying something new, being adventurous and in the most whimsical way.

It is charmingly illustrated in bright and happy colors.

Your child will want to read along and encourage the cow to do something different. Great fun!

HOW THE COW JUMPED OVER THE MOON may be found on Amazon as an e-book or soft-cover book -- http://amzn.com/B004WOWQXY.

If you liked *WHO NEEDS TEETH?* please be kind enough to post a short review on Amazon.

Receive a special Sally Huss children's e-book FREE by going to: http://www.sallyhuss.com/free.html.

More Sally Huss books may be viewed on the Author's Profile on Amazon. Here is that URL: http://amzn.to/VpR7B8.

About the Author/Illustrator

Sally Huss

"Bright and happy," "light and whimsical" have been the catch phrases attached to the writings and art of Sally Huss for over 30 years. Sweet images dance across all of Sally's creations, whether in the form of children's books, paintings, wallpaper, ceramics, baby bibs, purses, clothing, or her King Features syndicated newspaper panel "Happy Musings."

Sally creates children's books to uplift the lives of children and hopes you will join her in this effort by helping spread her happy messages.

Sally is a graduate of USC with a degree in Fine Art and through the years has had 26 of her own licensed art galleries throughout the world.

This certificate may be cut out, framed, and presented to any child who has demonstrated her or his worthiness to receive it.

Certificate of Merit

The child named above is awarded this Certificate of Merit for practicing good dental hygiene by:

*Brushing teeth twice a day
*Eating good and healthy foods
*Flossing (if applicable)
*Smiling often

(Name)

Presented by: _____ Date: _____

Made in the USA
Coppell, TX
01 November 2019